THIS CANDLEWICK BOOK BELONGS TO:

_____

_____

_____

_____

To Ginger,
Oti, and Diggy

Copyright © 1997 by Charlotte Voake

All rights reserved.

First U.S. paperback edition 2000

The Library of Congress has cataloged the hardcover edition as follows:

Voake, Charlotte.
Ginger / Charlotte Voake. — 1st U.S. ed.
Summary: When Ginger the cat gets fed up with dealing with his owner's new kitten,
it takes drastic measures to make the two of them friends.
ISBN 0-7636-0108-X (hardcover)
[1. Cats—Fiction.   I. Title.
PZ7.V855Gi   1997   [E]—dc20   96-20890
ISBN 0-7636-0788-6 (paperback)

2 4 6 8 10 9 7 5 3 1

Printed in Hong Kong

This book was typeset in Calligraphic.
The pictures were done in watercolor and ink.

Candlewick Press
2067 Massachusetts Avenue
Cambridge, Massachusetts 02140

GINGER

Charlotte Voake

CANDLEWICK PRESS

CAMBRIDGE, MASSACHUSETTS

Ginger was a lucky cat.

He lived with
a little girl
who made him
delicious
meals

and gave him
    a beautiful basket,

where he would curl up . . .

and close
his eyes.

Here he is,
fast asleep.

But here he is again,
WIDE AWAKE.

What's this?

A kitten!

"He'll be a nice new friend for you, Ginger," said the little girl.

But Ginger
didn't want a new friend,
especially one like this.
Ginger hoped the
kitten would
go away,

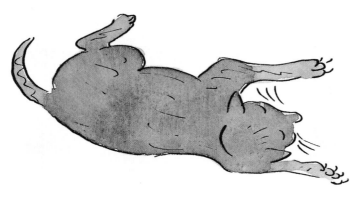

but he didn't.

Everywhere
Ginger went,
the kitten followed,
springing out
from behind
doors,

leaping onto Ginger's back,

even eating
Ginger's food!

What a naughty
kitten!

But what upset Ginger
more than anything
was that whenever
he got into his
beautiful basket,
the kitten always
climbed in too,

and
the little
girl didn't
do anything
about it.

So Ginger decided to leave home.

He went out
through the cat flap
and he didn't come back.

The kitten waited for a while,
then he got into
Ginger's basket.

It wasn't the same without Ginger.

The kitten
played
with some
flowers,

then he found somewhere to sharpen his claws.

The little girl
found him on the table
drinking some milk.

"You naughty kitten!" she said.

"I thought you
were with Ginger.
Where is he anyway?"

She looked
in Ginger's
basket,

but of course he wasn't there.

"Perhaps he's eating his food," she said.

But Ginger wasn't there either.

"I hope he's not upset," she said.

"I hope he hasn't run away."

She put on her
galoshes and
went out
into the
garden,
and that
is where
she found
him;

a very wet,
sad, cold Ginger,
hiding under
a bush.

The little girl carried Ginger and the kitten inside. "It's a pity you can't be friends," she said.

She gave Ginger a special meal.

She gave the kitten
a little plate
of his own.

Then she tucked Ginger
into his own
warm basket.

All she could find for the kitten to sleep in was a little tiny cardboard box.

But the kitten didn't mind, because cats love cardboard boxes (however small they are).

So when the little girl
went in to see
the two cats
again,

THIS is how she found them.

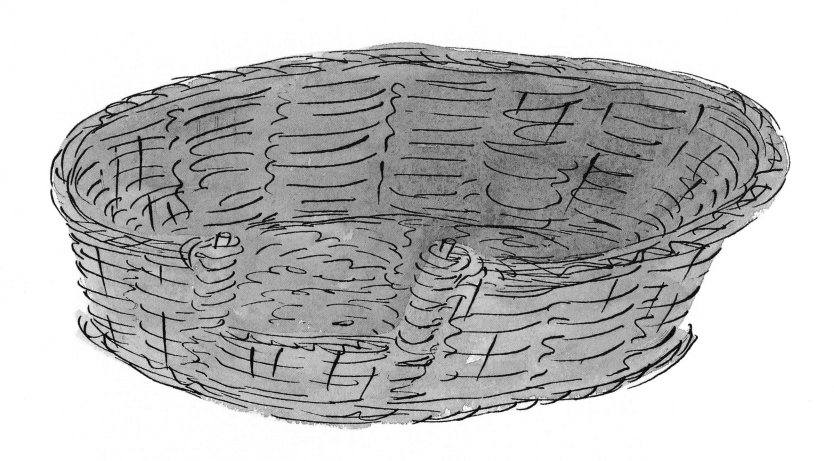

And now Ginger
and the naughty kitten
get along very well . . .

most of the time!

CHARLOTTE VOAKE says this story is "completely true. Our older cat's nose was seriously put out of joint when we brought a kitten home. But eventually they became absolutely inseparable." Charlotte Voake's stature as an illustrator has grown steadily throughout her career. With publication of *Ginger*, her delicate art and affectionate humor reach new heights.